Diary of an
Angry Alex: Book 8

By **Crafty Nichole**

Contents

Contents

Day One Hundred and Twenty-Four

5:00am

Evil wakes up early. At least, that's what Herobrine says. I hope that he'll be a better master than enemy. Ever since he made me his student, I'm not so scared of him anymore. Why was I ever scared of him? He still snores, and he's still a big, ugly jerk, but once we started really talking, we have a lot in common. Did you know that he had braces as a kid? Imagine that— an evil genius like him going to see the orthodontist.

Well, in any case, today is my first day of evil lessons, and I don't want to be late. I may not be scared of Herobrine, but that doesn't mean that I want to make him angry.

9:00am

So, the morning's lesson is pretty simple, or at least I thought it would be. How an evil genius gets food. It seemed easy enough and boring. I started fixing up my farm—you know, the one that got all trampled by spiders and donkeys and wolves. Well, I was working on it, and Herobrine hit me! He took a stick and whacked me over the head! Apparently, it isn't evil to grow your own food. At least, it isn't evil enough.

Herobrine destroyed the rest of the farm and now we're going to head out to the nearest village. It's one that I haven't been to before. I'm not sure what Herobrine wants to do there, but it can't be anything good. I'm so excited!

12:20pm

He's a jerk! Okay, that's not a surprise. But he is! A big one! We got to the village and all of the villagers were a little scared. I guess Herobrine had been there before. Then Herobrine starts threatening the villagers and hitting them with his stick. He didn't hurt them. Not really. But he's such a big bully! He hit them until the farmers gave him all their crops and the butcher gave him all his meat. We have enough food for at least a few days. Well, maybe less with the way that Herobrine eats. And Bucky. And Cloud. And Rudolph. I can make some hay bales for the four-legged ones. Herobrine should be fine with the meat. I can make the carrots and potatoes last for myself, but Herobrine's going to need more meat. I'm not sure how he eats so much of it, but maybe that's another part of being an evil genius.

Oh, that's right. Bucky doesn't really like Herobrine; I guess it's closer to hatred. Rudolph doesn't really mind him, though. Cloud won't even go near him. I think it's something about the way he smells, because her nose always goes funny when he comes around. Herobrine has his zombie horse to ride, but that won't work out during the daytime. I know that he wants to ride Rudolph for now, but I just can't let him. Rudolph is my evil steed. Herobrine can find his own.

When I told him that, he just stared at me with those fiery eyes. For a second, I thought he was going to hit me with his stick again, but I guess being possessive of your things is evil enough that he just nodded. I think he might really be starting to respect me.

7:30pm

We're back at the snow cabin for now. I know that he would never admit to it, but I think Herobrine doesn't have anywhere else to go. But it's nice to relax at home after a long day of shaking down villagers for wheat and pork.

Oh, the villagers. I let my conscience get the better of me a little bit. All I could think of was the long days working on Steve's farm while he was off mining. Why should some people have to do all the work

3

while others have all the fun?

I tried saying something to Herobrine about it, but he just hit me with the stick. He told me in his scary voice that I'm not allowed to think like that anymore. I wanted to snatch the stick out of his hand and beat him with it, but what can I do? He's still so much stronger than me. I guess I have a lot more to learn about being evil.

It's strange. I'm still angry—really, really angry—with Herobrine for not listening to me, but he said that we had another lesson after dark when the monsters come out. I'm not sure what he has in mind, but I'm excited. That's strange, isn't it?

Day One Hundred and Twenty-Five

4:00am

Spiders! It was spiders! Herobrine wants to teach me how to ride spiders, the way that the skeletons do. This way, we can have evil steeds during the daytime and I won't have to let him ride Rudolph. I guess evil geniuses know how to compromise. I'm not very good at it, though. It's going to take a lot of practice.

The spiders were really scary. Their bristles stabbed through my pants and prickled my legs. I'm going to need to make some leather riding pants if I'm going to be able to ride them anymore.

At least the monsters leave me alone now. That's something new that I like a lot about being evil: hanging out with skeletons. Sure, they're not great at conversation, but they're good teachers.

Now it's time to get a few hours of sleep before the next lesson later today. I wonder what Herobrine could have in store for me.

9:00am

That awful, evil tyrant woke me up so early. I can barely keep my eyes open. The only reason I woke up at all is because he dumped a bucket of water on my head. Not going to lie, I shouted at him after that. He just hit me with the stick and said I was lucky that it wasn't a bucket of lava. Tyrant. That's a fitting title. I better not call him that to his face though. I'm afraid he might like it.

1:30pm

This time it was a lesson about setting things on fire. Herobrine handed me a flint and steel and told me to start burning stuff. Well, I say stuff. He smacked me every time I wasn't being evil enough with my fire. He only seemed really satisfied with me when I tried to set Cloud on fire, but I couldn't do it. She didn't hold still long enough. I'm glad, though. I'd feel bad if I hurt her, even just a little bit. I tried telling Herobrine that I didn't want to set her on fire. He hit me with a log that time.

2:00pm

Herobrine has gone completely nuts! He keeps chasing me around, throwing flint and steel at me, and

6

yelling at me to burn more things! He just—OUCH! There's no getting away from this guy!!!

3:30pm

What have I done? The only thing that finally got that maniac to calm down was to set my cabin on fire. My cabin. My lovely cabin with the magenta roof...

I guess it just wasn't evil enough. I know that magenta isn't a terribly scary color, but I worked really hard on that cabin! Well, there isn't much left of it now... The farm got trampled in the big fight a couple days ago, and now there are only scorch marks left where my home used to be.

I know that Herobrine wants to move on. He says that we have to go someplace more evil. The lava lake in the jungle is one option, but I don't want to go there. Steve might still be in that area anyway. Maybe I should check in and see what he's up to. I'm sure Rudolph would like the exercise. Or it could be a good time to practice my spider-riding skills.

3:34pm

Nope, no spider riding for me. I'm not good at it and now I'm covered in spider bites. And then I accidentally killed my spider. Well what was I supposed to do? It didn't like the way I was riding and wouldn't stop biting me!

It doesn't matter. Rudolph will work just as well. I better get off and away before Herobrine tries to set more things on fire. Like me. I'd like to continue not being on fire.

5:00pm

Rudolph is doing well. He's a bit grumpy, but that's okay. I don't think any of my steeds like Herobrine all that much, especially with all the fire. We haven't gotten to Steve yet, but I think that I should build a little stable for Bucky and the rest somewhere around here. Someplace secret where Herobrine wouldn't think to look for them. I'll keep it in the back of my mind. For now, I want to check up on Steve.

8:30pm

Steve isn't at the lava jungle. I don't really know where he could be, but I know where to start looking. The villagers should have some idea of where he went.

11:30pm

Well, the villagers are all asleep for the night. The monsters won't bother me, so I'm going to camp out here and wait for morning.

Day One Hundred and Twenty-Six

9:00am

He was there! Steve's staying in the village, I mean. He's staying with the baker. No one seems too happy with him being around. It looks like he never learned any manners since back when he was bossing me around. He'll never just grow up and do his own chores. And from the way the baker was shouting at him, it looks like he never learned how to do any cooking either. I'm on my way back to Herobrine now. There's no reason to stick around spying on him. He isn't up to anything serious over here.

12:30pm

Well, I got back and Herobrine left me a note. A sign post, actually. He's setting up a base in the Nether. I guess that's the only place evil enough for him to have a base. I should say, "For *us* to have a base," but it still doesn't feel real. It's only the third day of my evil training. I can't ride spiders and I don't really like setting things on fire. Maybe there will be something else evil that I'll be good at.

Anyway, Herobrine left directions to find a Nether portal. Before I go, I'm going to set up the stable. I'll put it in the plains where I found Cloud. It might not be an evil thing to do, but I think they'll like it.

7:45pm

It took a while, but I got the stable built and I finally found the portal. Whatever else they are, evil geniuses are really bad at directions. Herobrine might be mad that it took me so long to get back to him. Maybe not though. There's no way to keep track of time in the Nether. Maybe he just hasn't noticed how long I've been gone?

7:51pm

I was wrong. He's mad.

11:25pm

Angry Herobrine is a scary thing. He didn't shout or hit me; he just got really quiet, staring at me with those flaming eyes. I wonder if I'll get fiery eyes when I turn into an evil genius...

It doesn't matter. Herobrine told me to go and rest. He has plans for tomorrow. He won't tell me what, but it should be exciting.

11

Day One Hundred and Twenty-Seven

???am

It's hard to say what time it is right now. I was resting on a gross, squishy bed of netherrack when Herobrine got my attention by setting fires all around me. I started choking on smoke before I even realized. He almost burned up my diary!

Well, I guess it doesn't matter. No harm, no foul; be a bigger person. All that stuff. Aw, forget all that nonsense. I'm furious! I get that he's evil and all, but does he have to be such a big jerk? To me??? I'm supposed to be his apprentice! How dare he?

Ahhh, okay. I'm calming myself down. It's going to be a good day. An evil day. A good evil day. I have to go meet Herobrine for our lesson.

12:00pm

Well, Herobrine says it's about noon right now. That's fine I guess. I thought it was earlier, but I have trouble telling time here. There's no sun and the lava keeps a steady amount of light. It doesn't matter.

Since I'm pretty much a student for real now, Herobrine let me ask any questions that I wanted to ask. I thought it would be a good time to work on my evilness and really start looking the part. My first question was how I could get my eyes to glow like his do. He told me that the only real way is to hold my head inside of a bucket of lava for long enough. I asked, "Long enough for what?" but he just hit me with that stick again. I don't really like being a student.

Maybe I'll try the bucket of lava out later. Herobrine has something else in mind for a lesson today.

6:00pm-ish

Well if I was furious before, I don't even have a word for how angry I am now. Enraged, maybe? Outraged? Definitely something with rage.

The lesson started okay. Herobrine asked what other evil things I have problems with, and I told him about how my evil plans never seem to work out. And it was all fine! Herobrine took me out to a Nether fortress and told me that there was a secret to always having a great evil plan: just don't make a plan. He says that the only thing that an evil genius has to have is a goal. As long as you keep your eyes on the prize and don't give up, things should work out. Plans only ever get in the way.

It made sense when he said it. That's why Steve and I always lost and Herobrine always won. Of course, after he said that, he told me that we were going to take over the Nether fortress. Then he said that I had to do it alone, and that I wasn't allowed to make a plan, I just had to go in there and do it. So I tried. I still had some armor and weapons from before, so I charged in.

I died. It was horrible. I got withered by a skeleton and set on fire by a blaze; I guess that even if I'm evil, I'll still get attacked if I get in the monsters' territory. That's good to know. Well, I burned to death and woke up all the way back at my original spawn.

And you'll never guess what was waiting for me at spawn! It was Steve! That terrible, jerkface jerk was there, probably to gloat. He started trying to talk to me about not being evil and that it was better to be good or whatever. I couldn't handle it. I lost it and started hitting him with my bare fist. Even without a weapon, it was just good to hit something. He was wearing armor, though, and I didn't hurt him at all. After a while, he just walked away. Gahh, he makes me so angry! Why doesn't he just fall in a hole already?

But I had to get back to the portal. I called Bucky to me with a good donkey laugh and rode back here. Hmm, maybe I should have asked Herobrine for help with my laugh first instead of the plans. Well, even if he does help me fix up my laugh, I should hang on to this donkey laugh too. It's pretty useful, and it could be a great secret weapon.

It doesn't help to be this angry. And when I got back, Herobrine had taken all of my things and stored them in a chest for me. That doesn't seem too evil, does it? Maybe he has a softer side. I said something like that to him, though, and he said that he obviously wasn't hitting me hard enough. The stick is going away for now. He's going to keep hitting me with the log though. At least it isn't as bad as him dropping lava on my head.

What a day, though. I hate dying almost as much as I hate that jerkface Steve. I'm so tired, but there's no way to sleep in the Nether without blowing up. Maybe I'll ask Herobrine if I can make a bed in the Overworld, somewhere close to the portal.

6:42pm

I asked him. He hit me in the head with the log. I guess I'll just eat my potatoes and have a bit of rest. It will have to do for now.

Day One Hundred and Twenty-Eight

8:36am

I hate having to ask Herobrine what time it is constantly, but it is just too difficult for me to tell here. I wonder how he knows what time it is...

Anyway, resting didn't turn out to be too restful. I'm still too angry to relax. And my head still hurts. I did get to talk to some lovely zombie pigmen, though. They're not great at talking, and their breath is just terrible, but they're okay company. Oh, who am I kidding? They're awful. All of this is just awful. Being evil is incredibly boring so far.

9:30am

In the meantime, I asked if there was any way to make my evil laugh any better. Herobrine had some suggestions. He agreed with me that it's hard work. That makes me feel a little bit better. But I'm not sure that I understand what he was talking about. He said that I should pretend that my whole body is full of bees and that the only way to get them out is to shout loud enough to scare them, but smile the whole time. Screaming and laughing seem like two different things to me, but well, that might be one of the reasons that I'm not really an evil genius.

Anyway, I tried laughing the way he said (MWAAA HAAAAA AAAAAAHHHHHH) and a whole swarm of fire bats swooped in and attacked us! Herobrine didn't seem to mind all that much, but I have some new burns that still hurt. Maybe if I try putting my head in another bucket of lava, I won't get hurt anymore.

9:40am

Nope. Just made the burns worse. Ouch. Fall in a hole, Herobrine.

10:25am

Well then. Herobrine says that I need to start practicing my evil skills. His suggestion was to start messing with the zombie pigmen. Sure, whatever. Sounds like a plan. No, never mind. Evil geniuses don't make plans. But I'll be out harassing the pigmen for a while. They smell bad, so they deserve it. Whatever kind of logic you want to use.

3:30pm

You know, there are only so many things I can do to annoy the zombie pigmen before feeling like a complete jerk. Sure, they fight back if you attack them directly, but if you just try to annoy them, they don't seem to care. And the little ones get their feelings hurt so easily.

I talked to Herobrine about it, but he just told me that the log obviously wasn't strong enough and then he dropped an anvil on my head. An anvil! Do you know how heavy those things are? Because I do! I almost died again! Why does he have to be such an awful tyrant? He and Steve deserve each other.

8:00pm

"No rest for the wicked." Well, that's more than just an expression to Herobrine. We're going to spend the night fighting our way through the Nether fortress to make it into our evil lair. With all the lava and scary architecture, it will definitely work out.

I'm just worried that it will go even worse than last time. My helmet and leggings were destroyed in my last shot at taking over the fortress. I can't really tell Herobrine that I'm worried, though. It isn't evil to worry about things like that. I don't plan on getting any more anvils dropped on my head.

10:25pm

We're really doing it. We've cleared all of the blazes out of the top level. Herobrine is super scary—more than I realized. He doesn't seem too bothered by being on fire. Maybe that's something else that he can teach me how to do. Or maybe he just has a good supply of fire resistance potions. Either way, I want to know his secret.

I took a short break to get my strength back and let some of my wounds heal. But now I need to get back to the fight.

Day One Hundred and Twenty-Nine

4:15am

It's been a hard couple of hours, but we finally took over the fortress. Herobrine even gave me a compliment! He liked the way that I fought. I didn't have a plan, but I was smart about it, taking chances but not unnecessary risks. Of course, then he lectured me for an entire hour about how to be better. Better, better, always better! I did a good job! Why is he so mean about it?

It doesn't matter. I need to get real sleep. It's been too long. I can't go back anywhere in the Overworld; all of my old beds have been destroyed. Maybe I can sneak away sometime and build a new one. Even if I'm gone for a long time, at least I'll have a bed and be able to sleep for real.

7:30am

Herobrine caught me trying to sneak out of the Nether. I lied and told him that I just wanted to go get some better evil practice, and Herobrine agreed with me. He said that it was time to get out and do some real evil. We're going to head out and see what the villagers have been up to since we went away. I told him that Steve was there too, and he got this really scary expression. It was just the most evil smile that I've ever seen. I almost feel bad for Steve. Almost.

9:10am

Herobrine is insisting on riding spiders to get to the village. I want to ask him if I can just ride Rudolph or Bucky instead. You know what? I will ask. I'm still no good at spider riding. It should be fine to do it my way. He liked the way that I fought. Why should this be different?

9:15am

I asked. He just looked at me with his scary eyes and pulled out the anvil. I think I might just try riding the spider this time. Who knows, maybe I'll be okay at it this time.

2:00pm

I'm not okay at this. It's taking forever to get there and I can feel Herobrine getting mad at me. I can't help it! I need more practice, sure, but if he would just let me ride Bucky instead, then we could have been there by now!

5:00pm

Well, we're here. Finally. Herobrine isn't saying much, but I can feel how much he's looking forward to attacking Steve. And that he's still grumpy about my terrible spider riding skills. I told Herobrine about all of the ways through the walls, so that's at least giving him something else to think about. It takes a lot of the heat off of me, anyway. And, it changes our tactics. With the new sandstone walls, we can't use spiders, but these holes and doors…Well, they're much easier to get through. Much easier to get an army through. Oh yes. As soon as the sun goes down, we're going out to find an army.

It seems like the perfect time to practice my evil laugh! BWAAHH HA HAAAA HAHAHAHAAA!!!

5:10pm

I think I did it! There doesn't seem to be a giant horde of anything running towards me. There aren't any donkeys or fire bats or anything like that! It's finally worked! I've made my first step at being a real evil genius!

I should find a bucket of lava to put my head in! Quick!

5:15pm

Never mind. Just, never mind. The lava burned me almost to death and I ran for the river to put myself out. There were all these squids flopping around, trying to get to me from the water. My new evil laugh makes squids come to me. This is just getting pathetic. Is there anything less evil than a squid?

8:00pm

I'm ready for the attack now. I'm all done playing around at being evil; it's time to be a real villain now. Herobrine went out to recruit a bunch of zombies to march through the west door, and I've got a bunch of skeletons over on my side. We're going to lead both of these armies to the village and let them loose. I only have about fifteen skeletons. I hope it's enough. When I leave them alone for too long, they start attacking each other. Oh, whoops. Down to thirteen skeletons. I better get them moving before I lose more of them.

11:00pm

Herobrine led the zombies in first, and then I brought in the skeletons. The villagers were already inside for the night, and the zombies got to work breaking down the doors. Steve rushed out of the baker's house and fought them off the best that he could. He killed a lot of them before they killed him the first time. He ran out again to try to get his stuff back, but the skeletons shot him full of arrows before he could get too close.

All of the blood ran to my head and I lost it. With my flint and steel, I ran out and started burning down some of the buildings. All of the wood parts, anyway.

Herobrine just watched me. He stood up on top of the wall, and he watched me burn the village to the ground. Some of the monsters burned up along with the wood, but I guess the cool part of being evil is that you don't have to worry about any of the evil hench-men that work for you.

I wish Herobrine would just say something to me. All he did was stare down from the wall with his crazy, burning eyes. I can't tell if he's incredibly powerful or if he's just a showoff. Maybe that lava bucket stuff is true, or maybe it's just one of his evil pranks to get me to dump lava on my head all the time.

Day One Hundred and Thirty

5:25am

Back in the Nether, Herobrine started talking again. Finally. He said that he had some kind of errand to take care of in the Overworld. I tried asking what kind of errand, but he just dropped the anvil on my head and left before I could even shout at him about it. I'm really starting to hate that guy again. Just the way that he treats me! Does he really think that he can just get away with that?

I'm cool…I'm calm. I let out a good bee-scream/ laugh over the lava pit and decided it's for the best. If Herobrine is going to be sneaking around, then so will I! Following him would probably only get me another anvil-shaped dent in my skull, so I'll go someplace else instead. Maybe I'll go visit the stable and make myself a bedroom there. Yes, that sounds like a great idea.

Of course, my laugh still isn't the greatest. My laugh brought a whole bunch of blazes flying down from who knows where. I ran away. I'm getting really, really tired of being set on fire, setting myself on fire, and just being on fire in general.

9:06am

I made it out to the stable. I didn't see any trace of Herobrine the whole way here, so I think it's safe enough. I don't have any blocks to build with, so I'm going to do a bit of digging and get some cobblestone. I don't trust wood so much anymore. Things have a habit of catching on fire whenever Herobrine or I get involved.

Plus, I'm not sure of how it works, but if this whole bucket of lava trick is for real, then my new fire eyes might be able to set things on fire. I don't know if that's what Herobrine does, but I wouldn't be surprised.

1:00pm

The room is finished. All I need is to gather some wool for the bed. Also, I ran out of potatoes during the attack last night, and I'm pretty close to starving. Working on no sleep and no food isn't helping my mood. I heard some sheep a little way from here. It shouldn't take too long to get some wool. I'll be able to get the bed set up before it gets dark.

I'll get in some laugh practice in the meantime. HEE HA BWA HA HAHAHAAA!!!

1:07pm

I took off running. Creepers! That time, it was creepers. I sprinted away before they could blow up my stable. I'm so tired of all of this! Why do I fail at being evil? Ugh. Maybe I should just fall in a hole and be done with all of this.

Whoa, whoa. Calm down Alex. Getting mad at yourself isn't very evil. Get mad at something else instead. I just need to find these sheep. Killing them should help calm me down.

2:30pm

Where are these sheep? I don't remember exactly where they were, but it should be around here somewhere.

3:00pm

Okay, where are they???

6:00pm

WHERE ARE THESE FREAKING SHEEP???

8:00pm

I found them. I killed so many. Enough for about five beds. Ahh, that feels better. I have the wool, so I should head back. I'm pretty close to the Nether portal now, so I'll just go back there for now. I hope Herobrine isn't back yet.

8:30pm

He's back. And he looks mad.

11:00pm

He was mad. He shouted at me for a long time about all the time that I wasted. Isn't that kind of funny? He wasted all that time yelling about wasting time. Well, it would be funny if I wasn't completely furious.

But he was mad that I wasn't working on being evil. I told him that I needed to sleep if I was going to get any better at anything. He laughed and dropped his anvil on my head. Apparently sleep is for the weak.

Well, I'll show him. I'll get all the sleep I need. I have the wool I need. I'll make a bed and sleep in it and then I'll show him just how smart I am when I'm well rested!

11:08pm

I didn't forget that beds explode in the Nether. Ignore the scorch marks on the page. That's from a completely different explosion.

Well, forget the bed. I feel completely awake now anyway. I guess I'll go try to make Herobrine happy and get some practice being evil for a while. Maybe if I keep him in a good mood, he'll stop trying to give me brain damage with all of these anvils.

11:30pm

Well, I guess it's as good a time as any to try out the lava bucket. I know that it probably won't work, but Herobrine told me to keep at it.

11:35pm

My face is on fire and Herobrine can fall in a hole.

Day One Hundred and Thirty-One

9:30am

Herobrine's been gone for a few hours. I'm not sure where he went, but he's missing some great evil over here. I tricked one of the pigmen into walking off a cliff and he fell in a huge pool of lava. I stole one of the little one's gold nuggets and now all the young ones are fighting, chasing each other all over the place. I traded out three of the pigmen's swords, and they're still arguing about whose is whose. Such great mayhem.

But seriously, where is Herobrine?

11:00am

He just got back. I was busy throwing bits of cobblestone at a ghast that got caught in a waterfall of lava. A waterfall? Should I call it a lavafall? It doesn't matter. I'm going to see Herobrine now.

11:30am

That tyrant, that maniac, that jerk! He can fall into the deepest pit of lava in this dump and just drown there. I'm so tired of his attitude. I just wanted to know where he's been going, if it's something I can help with or something that could help make me more evil—anything that I should know about. Of course, I didn't get more than the first, "Where were you?" before he pulled out the anvil again. When will I learn?

No. No, you know what? I'm done. It doesn't do enough to take all of my anger out on the zombie pigmen. They aren't what I'm mad at. I'm mad at Herobrine. He's the one I should be directing all of my evil towards. I'll figure out a way to get him. He may be my master, the evilest of all evil geniuses, but I'm done playing nice with him. I'm done with the games and the laughs and the buckets of lava to the face. I never should have listened to him in the first place! Just what makes him so great?

No, it's payback time, and I think I have a plan. I know that he said that evil geniuses don't plan, that they just get in the way and go wrong, but forget that. Forget everything that tyrant ever said. I'm going to be a much better evil genius. I'm going to have my own rules and keep doing things my way. And no one is going to change my mind about that anymore. He wanted to make me evil? Well he did. It feels good too!

2:00pm

I have everything ready. What I'm going to do is get a fishing rod and drag a bunch of ghasts over to Herobrine. They're one of the few things that always attack him on sight. There's pretty much only the ghasts and the withers. But where am I supposed to find one of those on short notice?

It doesn't matter. I know where the ghasts tend to hang out, and I'll be waiting there. It shouldn't take too long for one or two to wander over. It's a good thing that I'm such an amazing fisherman. I mean, I only learned how to fish in the first place to get away from Herobrine. It's fitting that I can use my fishing skills to take him out.

6:30pm

Why do I fail at life? Especially when I'm just trying to show my old master that I'm the better evil mastermind. My plan was so simple!

Revenge Plan:

- Hook ghasts on fishing rod over and over (and don't get blown up)

- Drag them towards the evil lair (still, don't get blown up)

- Get them to blow up Herobrine instead

- Run away as fast as possible

Everything was going well, but then I messed it all up because I fail at life. I tripped and my fishing rod broke, and the ghast that I was pulling back to the lair attacked me. I managed to kill it, but I've got to find more this time. I should make more than one fishing rod, also. It's going to work. I refuse to fail again. Ever again. I'll become unstoppable.

11:25pm

I did it! I got two ghasts all the way back to our base without getting blown up (too badly). I got them all the way there, and Herobrine was gone again! Where does he keep going? This is getting ridiculous! I had to kill the ghasts and now I'm just sitting around, waiting for stupid Herobrine to get back from his stupid, secret errands. I'm so tired. So, so, sooooo tired, and this is just too much for me.

Day One Hundred and Thirty-Two

10:00am

I feel much better. Instead of sitting around and sulking, I left the Nether. I put down a bed in the stable and slept through the night for the first time in such a long time. I'm still so angry, and very evil, but I feel like I'm thinking straight for the first time since those first days at the snowy cabin.

I have to destroy Herobrine, and I have to plan it out very carefully. I think I've got the perfect way to do it, too. Now that I know that I can catch the ghasts and drag them to wherever I need them, I can use that as a part of my plan.

The rest of the plan is going to need a lot of TNT. I better try and see if I can get my creeper laugh to work. I don't know how much time I'll have to set this all up, but I've got to make sure that it's all in place before Herobrine gets back. I don't want to have to wait and hope that he just disappears another time.

12:30pm

I've tried a few of my laughs. The only thing that happened is that now there are a whole lot of bats flying around, angry that I woke them up during the daytime. I'm not really close to the water, so I don't think that any squids have heard me. I don't see any flopping around on the ground, anyway. I'll keep trying until I get some creepers to come back. I'm doing it just the same way that I wrote before, but they just aren't coming out.

Maybe I'll go to the beach and dig up some sand while I keep trying. At least squids aren't as annoying as bats.

3:00pm

This is another of those good news/bad news kind of times. The good news is that I think that I've got my creeper laugh down. The bad news is that I got blown up. A lot.

It's a good thing that I managed to sleep in that bed. If I'd been blown up without the bed set, my spawn point is too far away for me to recover my stuff. I almost lost this diary! I'm still in the stable. I think I'll leave the diary here and come back for it after I get all of the TNT I need for my plan to work.

Day One Hundred and Thirty-Three

2:30am

I have it. Almost half a stack of TNT. It took so long to get all of it, and my throat is pretty sore from all the laughing, but now it's time to get back to the evil lair. I hope Herobrine isn't there. I want to get my trap set up before he gets back.

Ah, yes! My new plan is much better!

Revenge Plan:

- Plant TNT in the lair under the floor

- Get Herobrine to wait for me close to the TNT

- Hook ghasts on fishing rod like before (and of course, don't get blown up)

- Drag them towards the evil lair (still, don't get blown up)

- Trick them into shooting fireballs at the TNT

- Run away before I get exploded

It has to work this time! It should be easy to make it

look like the ghasts blew him up. After I get him raging mad, I'll tell him that it was me all along, and then he'll be one of my evil henchmen forever! There's no way that he won't want to after he sees the extent of my evil genius! I'll show him once and for all that any good genius needs a good evil plan!

For now, I have to get back to the Nether portal. I can't wait to see the look on his face!

6:45pm

I know I said that I wanted to see his face, but only after I blew it up! He was already there when I got back, and I'm tired of waiting for him to leave again. Just go! Go away!!!

10:00pm

He's still here, so now I have to pretend that everything's still okay. I've got a bucket of lava, still. Maybe I should try making my eyes glow again? Man, I really don't want to.

10:02pm

YEP, IT STILL DOESN'T WORK BUT HOLY COW DOES THAT HURT!!!

Day One Hundred and Thirty-Four

2:30am

Herobrine told me that I'm too impatient, that I'll get my fire eyes when I'm ready. Well, fall in a hole already! I'm tired of his lectures and his ugly face and why won't he just leave already?

Oh wait, there he goes…

Time to put my plan into action! HahaHA HEE HWAA HAHAAAHAHA!!!

4:00am

That laugh brought a bunch of magma cubes bouncing over my way. It doesn't matter; those are easy enough to take care of.

I got the TNT all set up. I'm going to go play with the zombie pigmen until Herobrine comes back. Sure, they don't really like me too much, but there's no reason that we won't get along.

4:30am

I can't find the pigmen. I don't know where they went.

Maybe they saw me carry in all that TNT and got nervous. I can't say that I blame them. With Herobrine for a neighbor, maybe it's better to be a little bit careful. I know that I don't trust him even the tiniest bit and I live with him.

What else is there to do here? Not too much… I can't even sleep. By the time I get back to my bed in the Overworld, it'll already be daytime. I'm not about to suffer through the same taunting reminder of "you can only sleep at night" until I go crazy. No, I will wait here and when Herobrine gets back, I'm going to blow him up and drop him in the deepest, fieriest hole in all the Nether.

9:26am

He's here! Finally! I'm going to get him to the TNT room, and then I'll set the rest of the plan in motion. It's happening! It's really happening!

10:02am

I told him to wait, so he should be right where I left him. I have one ghast now, and I'm tugging it towards the lair. I don't even need to find another one. It should only take one fireball—OUCH! Okay, maybe it's not such a great idea to be writing while pulling this guy along with me.

10:34am

Something is wrong. I got the ghast to shoot directly at where the TNT should be, but nothing happened. No explosion, no dead Herobrine. I have a bad feeling about this…

I'll just go check on the TNT and see what the problem is.

7:25pm

What a day, what a day! A terrible, good-for-nothing, lousy, miserable, creeper fart of a day. My plan was so good. Too good! I should start at the beginning, I guess.

The ghast didn't do anything wrong. That part of the plan went exactly right. It shot a fireball into the exact right place, but the TNT wasn't there anymore. Herobrine had figured out that I was up to something. I guess that's the problem with my plans: they always feel too much like plans. He saw that I was acting differently and when I told him to wait, he knew it was a trap. He found the TNT and destroyed all of it.

So when I went to check and see what was wrong, there wasn't any TNT. Instead, Herobrine dropped a whole bunch of terrible silverfish on me, and I died right there. That wouldn't have been so bad if it had ended there. I would have spawned back at the stable and I'd have Bucky and Rudolph and Cloud still, and I could have made another fresh start somewhere else in the world.

But no, of course Herobrine wouldn't just let that happen. He was two steps ahead of me. For someone who doesn't make any evil plans, he sure is good at knowing how they work. I spawned back at my original spawn point, and I was confused, angry, and super disappointed. But mostly angry.

I sprinted back to the stable, and I was so sure that everything would be on fire. That's Herobrine's thing, anyway. It would have been better if it was all on fire. No, instead of that, I find that both Herobrine and Steve are waiting for me there.

They had a big sign made out of wool blocks that said, "INTERVENTION" and even Bucky, Rudolph, and Cloud were there. They all had these pieces of paper and they started telling me about how worried they were about me, about how my anger has been changing me, all that kind of stuff.

Well, except for the pack animals. They were just eating their papers. I guess that doesn't matter so much. The point is that they were there too. They must agree with that tyrant, Herobrine and that jerk, Steve.

Gosh, Steve! Why was that jerk even there? Why won't he just leave me alone? And how come he gets along with Herobrine all of a sudden? None of this is fair!

But apparently that's where Herobrine's been disappearing to this whole time! He's been sneaking out to meet with Steve so that they could do this stupid intervention.

Well I refuse! I'm not angry! I'm furious, but that doesn't mean that I have anger problems! I'm doing fine! I'll show them! I'll show everyone!

At least they gave me my diary back. They told me that there's going to be a villager coming soon to take me away and put me in a little village a long way from here, someplace peaceful where I can recover. Anger management. Can you believe it? Why doesn't everyone just find a nice hole to fall in and leave me alone? I like being evil! Just because I'm not good at it doesn't mean that I should give up.

The villager is here. I have to go now, but this isn't the end. You haven't seen the last of me!

To be continued…

To be continued...

Made in the USA
Coppell, TX
09 December 2024

42077581R00030